Mandy
Made Me Do It

JAN WEEKS

Illustrated by Janine Dawson

sundance

A Haights Cross Communications Company

The Story Characters

Mandy
Her little brother keeps getting her in trouble.

Tim
Mandy's little brother.

Mom
Mandy's mother.

The Story Setting

TABLE OF CONTENTS

CHAPTER 1

Tim the Troublemaker

My brother's name is Tim. He's four years old and gets into trouble all of the time. When he gets into trouble, he always blames **me**.

"Mandy made me do it," Tim says,
pointing at me.

So I get in trouble, too.

Mom says I should have more sense because I am the oldest.

I used to tell Tim to do things. But that was when I was six.

I don't do it anymore. Tim can think of bad things to do all by himself.

At breakfast, Tim poured the box of
cornflakes over his head.
The cornflakes went everywhere.

Then Tim pushed his head into the box and said it was his school hat. He doesn't even go to school.

When Mom saw the mess, she told
Tim he did a bad thing.

Tim stuck out his bottom lip and began to cry.

"Mandy made me do it," said Tim.
"She told me the cornflakes were
drops of rain and that I could make
a big storm."

Mom made **me** clean up the mess. It
was no use telling her I didn't do it.
The only person she believes is Tim.

CHAPTER 2

Beds Are Not Trampolines

After I finished cleaning up, I found Tim jumping on his bed. Mom had just made it.

The pillow was on the floor, and the blanket was crumpled.

"This is my trampoline," Tim said.

"You'll get into trouble," I answered.
"Mom told you not to jump on the
bed."

Tim began to jump higher.

"I bet I can touch the ceiling," he said. "Whee! This is fun!"

Tim did a super jump. Then he fell off the bed and landed on his nose. He started to cry.

Tim cried louder and louder.
Mom came running into the room
and picked him up.

"Now what have you done?" she asked, looking at his red nose.

"Mandy made me do it," Tim sobbed. "She told me I was Superman. She told me to jump off the bed."

Mom told Tim not to listen to me.
He had to think for himself.

Then she showed me her angry face.

The Next Day

I was brushing my teeth. Tim came into the bathroom. He had his boat in his hand.

"What are you doing?" I asked.

"Mom said I had to brush my teeth," said Tim.

He put the plug in the sink and turned on the faucet.

Tim put his boat in the water.
He started singing, "Row, row, row
your boat, gently down the stream!"

I went to get dressed for school.
When I came back, the sink was
overflowing. Tim was standing in a
pool of water.

Mom came in.

"Just look at you, Tim," Mom said.
"You're soaking wet!"

"Mandy made me do it," Tim said. "She told me my boat was a big ship sailing on the ocean. She said to make waves in the water."

"If Mandy told you to fly to the moon, would you do that, too?" Mom asked.

Tim nodded his head and said he did everything I told him. Then he smiled at me.

I was getting really tired of Tim.

CHAPTER 4

Visitors

On Thursday, our aunt and uncle were coming to visit. They were from the country, and we hadn't seen them for a long time.

"I want you both on your best behavior," said Mom.

Mom made a chocolate cake.

On the way home from school,
she stopped at the supermarket.

She bought some strawberries to put
on top of the cake.

"I love strawberries," Tim said. He was sitting in the backseat of the car. The strawberries were in his lap. "Strawberries are my favorite food."

"Just don't squash them," Mom said.

Mom put the strawberries in the fridge. When she went to use them, they were gone.

Tim was sitting on the floor with the
empty box. His mouth was red, and
he had strawberry juice all over his
face.

"Mandy made me do it," Tim said. "She told me the strawberries were magic. She said if I ate them everyone would give me presents."

I knew what I'd like to give him, and it wasn't a present.

Mom sent Tim to his room. He was to stay there until she told him to come out.

CHAPTER 5

Big Trouble

Mom was talking to our aunt and
uncle. They were having a good chat.

I went out to the backyard with a
bag of balloons. I wanted to make
some water balloons.

I had to push the balloon over the end of the hose and then tie a knot to keep the water in. It was a little tricky.

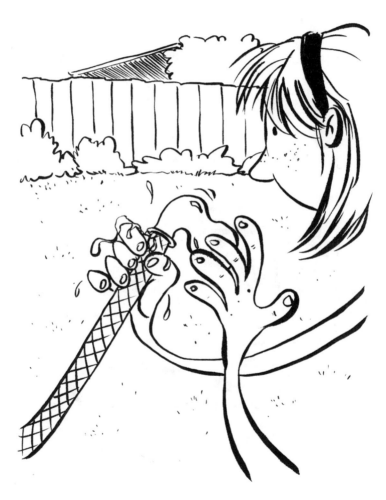

I could see Tim watching me from his bedroom. It would be great to throw one at him.

Then my friend Paul came over. He asked me to come look at his dad's new car.

When I came back, Tim was in **big** trouble. He had climbed out of his bedroom window to make a water balloon.

As Tim turned the water on,
his balloon flew off. Water sprayed
all over the yard.

Just then, Mom and Aunt Beth
stepped into the yard. Both of them
were sprayed with water. Boy, were
they angry!

My aunty's new dress was soaking wet.

Mom was wearing the angriest face you can imagine.

"Who are you going to blame this time?" Mom asked Tim. "You can't blame Mandy. She wasn't home."

"It was Daddy," he answered. "He made me do it."

And Dad was at work.

Mom looked at Tim. "I think we need to talk," she said.

GLOSSARY

 **behavior**
the way we act

blames
says someone did
something wrong

 **chat**
a friendly talk

crumpled
pressed out of shape

favorite
the one I like best

overflowing
spilling over
the top

soaking
very, very wet

sprayed
squirted a stream of water

supermarket
a big store with food

trampoline
a springy pad for
jumping and tumbling

Jan Weeks

Jan Weeks has written many poems, plays, songs, and stories for children. She is an experienced teacher with an interest in the development of sound reading skills and the promotion of literature. Jan is married and has three sons.

Janine Dawson

Janine loves to draw, in fact she loves to draw a lot — and swim, but never at the same time. She lives with her daughter, two cats, and a nervous goldfish.

Published by Sundance Publishing
P.O. Box 1326, 234 Taylor Street, Littleton, MA 01460

Copyright © text Jan Weeks
Copyright © illustrations Janine Dawson

First published 1999 as Sparklers by
Blake Education, Locked Bag 2022, Glebe 2037, Australia
Exclusive United States Distribution: Sundance Publishing

ISBN 0-7608-4940-9

Printed in Canada